For my Aunty Anwyl, who makes things grow – S.P.C.

*For my mother, Marja Lee Krüijt,
who has guided me through life's changing seasons* – V.L.

Persephone copyright © Frances Lincoln Limited 2009
Text copyright © Sally Pomme Clayton 2009
Illustrations copyright © Virginia Lee 2009

First published in Great Britain in 2009 by
Frances Lincoln Children's Books, 4 Torriano Mews,
Torriano Avenue, London NW5 2RZ
www.franceslincoln.com

British Library Cataloguing in Publication Data
available on request

ISBN: 978-1-84507-533-0

Illustrated with mixed media

Set in Galliard

Printed in Singapore

1 3 5 7 9 8 6 4 2

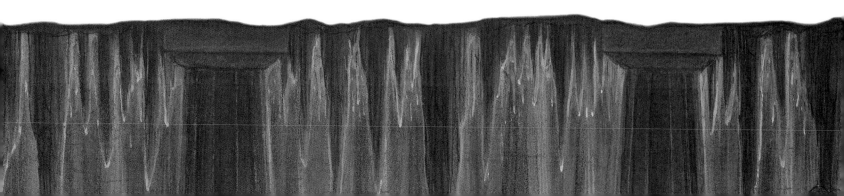

PERSEPHONE

A JOURNEY FROM WINTER TO SPRING

Sally Pomme Clayton

Illustrated by Virginia Lee

F

FRANCES LINCOLN
CHILDREN'S BOOKS

Persephone was playing in the fields, running,
laughing, chasing her friends. The sun was warm
on her bare arms, the long grass tickled her legs.
It was spring. Everything was growing. A feast
of flowers spread before her. She followed them,
greedy for their bright colours, gathering
blossoms into the folds of her gown.

Brilliant crocuses, violets like gems, narcissi
nodding their heads, green shoots of barley
pushing out of the ground – Persephone
picked and picked and picked,
leaving her friends far behind.

Suddenly there was a rumbling sound. The earth trembled and
the ground opened up. A golden chariot appeared, pulled by four horses,
black as night. Hades, King of the Underworld, shook the reins.

"Whoaa, my beasts! What beauty is this? A living girl to be my bride?"

And he reached out, plucked Persephone from the ground
and pulled her into his chariot.

"You will be Queen and light up my kingdom."

Persephone began to cry. But Hades cracked his whip
and the horses galloped off.

They rode and rode, until they came to a pool. A sparkling
spring of water bubbled up from underground – a gateway
to the Underworld. Hades pulled his horses to a stop.

But a water nymph with flowing hair and dripping dress
rose up from the pool.

"This is my home," she said. "No one enters here by force."
And she stretched out her watery arms to block their path.
"You cannot make this girl go with you."

But Hades threw his golden whip into the water. It struck
the bottom of the pool and a door appeared. Then Hades, chariot,
horses and Persephone hurtled down, down to the Underworld.

They raced along beneath towering rocks, past snakes and crawling creatures, beside boiling lakes, spouts of steam and smouldering fields of lava.

"Now you are Queen, all this belongs to you," said Hades.
"Look!" And he pointed to the earth shot through with glistening
seams of gold, to lumps of crystal winking beside the road.
But a shadow fell across Persephone's face, and stayed there.

Out in the sunshine, Persephone's friends stopped playing
and looked about. They saw a heap of flowers lying on the ground and their
laughter fell away. They ran to Persephone's mother, their words tumbling out.
"She's gone – Persephone's gone!"

Mother Demeter, Goddess of Earth, called and called, but there
was no reply.

So she took a burning torch in each hand and set off,
searching for her daughter. Demeter walked through long hot days
and frosty nights looking for Persephone. She walked and walked
for weeks and months, walked the whole Earth round,
but did not find her daughter.

Demeter came to a pool, sat down to rest, and saw
a ribbon floating on the water. She reached across,
pulled the ribbon out, and tears sprang from her eyes,
"This is Persephone's ribbon. I tied it in her hair
myself," cried the goddess. "Oh, where is my daughter?"

The water bubbled and the nymph rose up,
"Great Goddess, I know where your daughter is.
Hades has taken her to his kingdom. I swam down,
peeped into the Underworld and saw her sad face.
Persephone is Queen, sitting on a throne of gold –
but she neither eats nor sleeps, she only weeps."

"Curse you, cruel Earth," cried Demeter. "You don't deserve
to bear fruit if you keep my daughter underground."

Demeter pulled her cloak around her shoulders and a cold wind
began to blow. It tore leaves from trees and plants from roots.
The earth was frozen, hard as stone. Flowers, fruits and barley
lay hidden underground.

A year passed and nothing grew. It was a year of biting
hungry misery – winter all the time. No one recognised
the Great Goddess, wrapped in her cloak, weeping and
waiting for the world to die of hunger.

Father Zeus, God of Sky, looked down and saw that the Earth was dying. He called his swiftest messenger.

"Hermes, you travel the world, you know the way to every secret place. Find Persephone, bring her back. Then Demeter, Goddess of Growth, will make Earth green again."

Hermes put on his winged sandals and magic helmet,
took up his golden wand wound round with snakes,
and in a flash rose up into the air.

He flew, swift as wind, between sky and sea, like lightning
through clouds and over rock. In an instant he was underground,
in Hades' shady kingdom.

"I come with a message: Father Zeus calls Persephone home. Earth is dying. Nothing grows without her. Hades, you must let her go."

Hades was silent. Persephone held her breath, waiting for him to speak, and the Underworld waited too.

At last Hades said, "Persephone, flower of my life, you have made my gloomy kingdom bright. Everything shines while you are here. But because I love you, I will let you go. Let no one say that Hades is a cruel king. Go home, Persephone, be no longer sad."

Persephone leapt to her feet.

"Wait, my Queen," said Hades, lifting a golden plate piled
with juicy seeds. "All this time no food has passed your lips.
Please, eat before you go."

The seeds were red and seemed to glow. Persephone suddenly
felt hungry. She reached out, took three seeds and popped them in her
mouth. She crushed the seeds against her tongue and a sweet, tangy juice
burst inside her mouth. Persephone licked her lips.

Then Hermes took her hand and in an instant, swift as wind,
they flew from dark to light.

Demeter looked up – and there stood Persephone!

She flung her arms around her daughter, hugged her tight, then took the tattered ribbon and tied it in Persephone's hair. Mother and daughter clasped hands and walked home.

With each step Persephone took, the grass grew, buds opened, flowers bloomed and green shoots of barley pushed out of the earth. The air was filled with the sound of birds singing, for Persephone had returned – spring had come at last.

At home, Demeter spread the table with fresh bread,
white cheese, dark olives and cool glasses of barley water.
"It's so lovely to be home," laughed Persephone.
"I'm starving!" And she reached towards the food.
"You didn't eat, my daughter, did you?" asked Demeter.
"You didn't eat the food of the Underworld?"
"No Mother. No food passed my lips," said Persephone,
sucking on an olive stone. "Oh! Except..."
"Except what?" said Demeter.
"Three pomegranate seeds. Three tiny little seeds."

Demeter began to cry.

"Oh, Persephone! The food of the dead must not pass the lips of the living. For those three seeds, my daughter, I will lose you."

And so it is that for three months of each year Persephone must return to the Underworld. Hades welcomes back his queen, but when Persephone goes underground, winter comes to the Earth.

When the three months are over, Persephone returns. Ice melts, the ground grows soft,

Demeter hugs her daughter and spreads a feast of flowers. Earth bears fruit and we have spring.

Then Demeter can pick barley to make bread knowing, like all mothers, that for anything to grow it must winter underground, knowing that life depends on death, laughter on tears, and spring on winter.

Now, when you see a seed growing, a bud opening, a flower blooming, you too will know that all life depends on Persephone's journey.

A journey from death to life – about the story

In Ancient Greece, the goddesses Demeter and Persephone were honoured every year with festivals linked to the cycle of planting, growing and harvesting. One of the biggest festivals was held in the autumn, when women sowed seeds and asked Demeter to make the seeds grow and the harvest fruitful. The mysteries of Demeter also described the journey of growing up – in particular the journey a girl makes to become a woman and a mother. People took part in the festivals hoping to understand the secrets of the myth and to be renewed by them.

One of the most important moments of the celebration was when a priestess held up, for all to see, a stalk of barley – the mystery of life.

The Persephone myth is no longer part of religious
life in Greece, yet it still echoes through many everyday
customs. Pomegranate trees grow everywhere there,
and the fruit is still connected to both life and death.

On New Year's Eve, people crack pomegranates on
their doorsteps to bring good luck and prosperity for
the coming year.

At weddings, pomegranates are broken open and the
seeds rolled across the ground to bring a happy marriage
and lots of children.

At funerals, a special dish called *kollyva* is prepared in
honour of the dead. It is made from boiled wheat, sugar
and raisins, and decorated with pomegranate seeds.
Even gravestones are decorated with pomegranate fruits
and flowers.

The myth of Persephone links life and death in an
endless circle of regeneration.

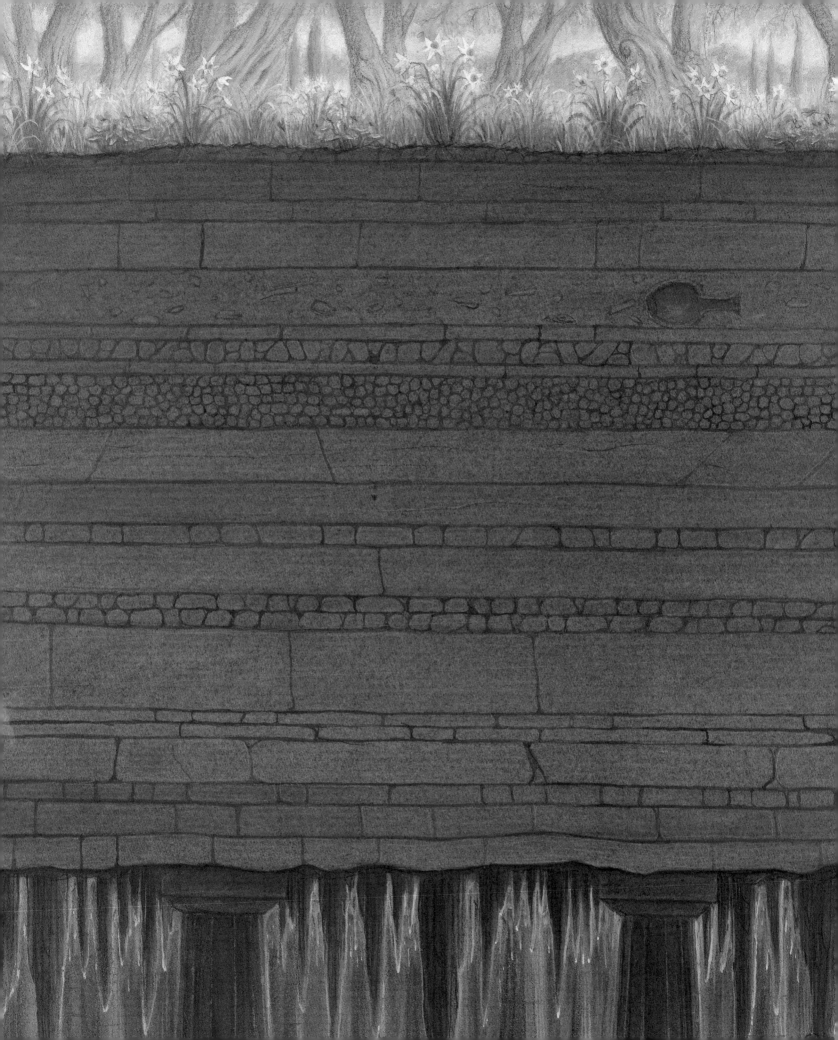